THE NATURE COMPANY

WILD SAFARI

**Photographs and Text
by Rick and Susan Sammon**

**Starrhill Press
Washington, D.C.**

Wild Animals of Africa

One of the best places in the world to see wild animals is Tanzania, a country in East Africa. There are more animals per square mile in Tanzania's Serengeti National Park than anywhere else on land.

When we visited the plains of the Serengeti, we saw thousands of wildebeests, hundreds of zebras and impalas, and dozens of lions and cape buffaloes. We also saw vultures, storks, and many other kinds of birds. And guess what? We saw all this before lunchtime on our first day in the park!

While we were on safari at Tanzania's Lake Manyara National Park, a family of elephants crossed the road right in front of our Land Rover. Moments later, the trees were alive with more curious baboons than we could count. When we were leaving the park, we passed 50 hippos taking a mud bath. The wriggling hippos were surrounded by hundreds of pink flamingos.

The most dramatic place we visited during our safari was Ngorongoro Crater, one of the largest volcanic craters on earth. As in most African habitats, the struggle of life and death in the animal kingdom happens here every day. But because the area is a protected national park, only animal predators hunt here.

Conservation groups all over Africa have helped set aside beautiful areas as national parks. In the parks, hunting is illegal. But just as importantly, their habitats are left undisturbed, except for a few dirt roads that don't seem to bother the animals.

The conservation efforts in East Africa and other protected parts of Africa will continue, thanks to governments, park rangers, and park managers—and thanks to the cooperation of local people. With their help, nature's incredible African creatures will survive in an ever-changing world.

Rick and Susan Sammon
Croton-on-Hudson, New York

The People of East Africa

Many East African natives are members of the Masai people. The Masai in the photo are two of the village elders, who are highly respected for their knowledge and wisdom. They are posing at the stick gate to their small village of about 20 people. At night the gate is closed to keep out lions.

The traditional Masai are cattle herders. They have to move their homes when all the grass is eaten. People who are on the move like the Masai are called nomadic.

For countless generations, the Masai have shared the grasslands with wild animals. The Masai respect all animals. They know that even lions, which sometimes kill their cattle, are important to the balance of nature. Young Masai boys must prove their courage by killing a lion with a spear. To accomplish this dangerous task, they hunt in a team with older villagers.

Some Masai leave their villages to work in the city, but many try to keep up their tradition of living close to nature. They have a great saying we can all understand: "Happiness is as good as food."

LIONS are called "kings of the jungle" because they have no natural predators. Like most of the animals that people see on safari, lions have become accustomed to vehicles. As a result, visitors can see one of the animal kingdom's fiercest hunters face to face. Lions are often seen sleeping or resting. That's because they sleep about 20 hours a day—if they've had enough to eat, that is.

PREY
Lions eat many kinds of animals, including zebras, impalas, giraffes, and wildebeests. The females in a group of lions usually do the hunting, while the male watches. After the prey animal is taken down, the male moves in for his meal.

PHYSICAL CHARACTERISTICS
Lions are the same light brown color as the grass of the open plains. When they crouch down, they're almost invisible. They're not very fast runners, so lions sneak up on their prey, surprising their victim before it has a chance to run away.

SCIENCE EXTRA
Lions catch prey because they hunt in teams. When they're walking in tall grass, lions sometimes raise their tails to show other lions where they are.

ZEBRAS

are the wild horses of Africa. Some people think zebras are white animals with black stripes. Others think they're black animals with white stripes. Take a look. What do you think?

PHYSICAL CHARACTERISTICS

Each zebra has a unique pattern of stripes, and the pattern is different on each side of its body. The reason for the stripes is still a mystery. Some experts think they help zebras blend together, so predators find it hard to spot a single animal. Others think the zebra uses its stripes to attract a mate, or that the stripes help baby zebras find their mothers.

PREDATORS

Dawn, dusk, and night are dangerous times for zebras. Lions and hyenas that hunt zebras are most active then. When zebras sense danger, they bunch together for protection.

FOOD

Zebras eat tall, coarse grasses. After the zebras move on, wildebeests eat the shorter grasses that are left over. Then gazelles feed on the remaining plant shoots.

FUN FACT

Zebras are born with brown stripes. As baby zebras get older, their brown stripes turn black.

GIRAFFES

GIRAFFES are the tallest animals in the world. They use their long necks to eat the leaves of tall trees. Giraffes live in herds of five to forty animals, but adult males usually live alone.

PHYSICAL CHARACTERISTICS

Each giraffe has a different pattern of spots on its chestnut-colored body. The animal's "horns" are actually round, fleshy knobs covered with skin.

PREDATORS

The giraffe's natural predator is the lion. But this graceful animal is also hunted by humans for its beautiful skin.

DEFENSES

Giraffes have strong leg muscles and hard hoofs. A kick from an angry giraffe can kill a lion. However, giraffes don't use their powerful legs when they fight each other. Instead, they bash their necks and heads together. This is called "head slamming" or "necking."

SCIENCE EXTRA

According to scientists, giraffes fall into a deep sleep lying down for only one hour a day. But they take shorter naps with their eyes half-closed while they're standing up. Napping giraffes snap awake if they hear a noise or sense danger.

ELEPHANTS

ELEPHANTS are the largest land animals. If you piled two small schoolbuses on top of each other, you'd have a double-decker bus that's about the same size and weight as an elephant. What's amazing is that elephants grow so big on a diet of small leaves and grass.

PHYSICAL CHARACTERISTICS

The African elephants shown in this book look different than their Asian cousins. African elephants are usually larger than Asian elephants, and their larger ears are shaped like fans. Male and female African elephants have huge tusks, but Asian females and some males have no tusks at all.

PREDATORS

The elephant's main predator is humans. People often illegally hunt these gentle giants for their ivory tusks. An adult male's tusk may be 12 feet long and might weigh more than 200 pounds. Natural predators like lions, leopards, and hyenas attack only baby elephants.

SCIENCE EXTRA

An elephant's skin is about one inch thick, which is much thicker than human skin. In fact, elephants are called pachyderms, which means "thick skin."

MARABOU STORKS

MARABOU STORKS stand four feet high and have a wingspan of more than eight feet. They can soar for long distances on thermals, which are warm air currents that rise upward and provide lift. Marabou storks usually take off on long flights between mid-morning and late afternoon, when thermals occur.

PHYSICAL CHARACTERISTICS

Even some bird lovers think the marabou is one of the ugliest storks. It has an unattractive, pink and fleshy pouch that dangles from its throat and a mostly bald head. But when it flies, the marabou stork is as graceful as a hawk.

PREY

Marabou storks are the main predators of pink flamingos. Marabou storks also eat the remains of dead animals that are left behind by carnivores like lions and cheetahs.

HABITAT

The marabou storks in this book were photographed on the southern rim of Ngorongoro Crater. This habitat is home to abundant bird life, including ostriches, flamingos, pelicans, crowned cranes, and eagles. Altogether, about half a million birds live on the crater.

IMPALAS are members of the antelope family. These animals are beautiful, whether they're running, jumping, or standing still. The impala's reddish brown coat reflects the golden sunlight. When it's frightened, the impala leaps gracefully into the air—sometimes as high as 10 or 12 feet. This mighty leap confuses predators and gives the impala a chance to run away.

HABITAT

Impalas are usually found in small herds around trees and grasslands. In the rainy season, they travel across the African plains and eat grasses, herbs, and the leaves of bushes and shrubs.

PREDATORS

Leopards and cheetahs are the main predators of the impala. But lions and hyenas also like to eat these fleet-footed antelopes—when they can catch them.

FUN FACT

When an antelope leaps into the air and comes down running, it's performing an activity called "pronking," which is a combination of running and jumping. You probably pronk like an antelope when you play outdoor games.

CHEETAHS are the fastest animals on four legs.

These big, athletic cats can run up to 70 miles per hour in short bursts. That's faster than the legal speed limit on highways. There are only a few animals speedier than cheetahs, such as hawks or swifts in flight.

PREDATORS

The fur of the cheetah is prized on the illegal market. Humans who hunt the animal illegally are the cheetah's main predator.

PREY

Cheetahs usually stalk young antelopes in the early morning and late afternoon—times of day when it's not too hot to hunt. During the hottest part of the day, they nap in the shade.

PHYSICAL CHARACTERISTICS

Cheetahs have tawny hair that's covered with black spots of various sizes. You can recognize a cheetah by the two black stripes under its eyes that look like they were made by falling teardrops. The vertical black stripes help hide the cheetah's face when it's looking through the grass at prey.

FUN FACT

Although a cheetah can sound like a barking dog, the most common sound it makes is like a chirping bird.

WILDEBEESTS

WILDEBEESTS might be the strangest-looking animals in Africa. They have horns like buffaloes, long beards, and floppy manes. When they run, they sometimes flop their heads from side to side in a comical manner. Because of the way they look, they're known as the "clowns of the plains."

HABITAT
Wildebeests are constantly searching for food and water. In the springtime, as many as one million wildebeests migrate almost 1,000 miles, following the African rainy season.

PREDATORS
Lions are the main predators of young wildebeests. But fenced-in ranchlands are also a threat, because wildebeests eat the same food as livestock. In some African countries, wildebeests are dying because they can't find enough open grazing land. But more than a million wildebeests live in the Serengeti, where the habitat is protected.

SCIENCE EXTRA
Wildebeests are always moving toward rain. Scientists know these animals can detect rain when it's still 30 miles away, but they don't know how the wildebeests do it.

Photograph © David G. Burder

BABOONS

BABOONS are the largest monkeys in the world. They're called "opportunistic feeders." This means that baboons eat whatever is available when they're hungry—plants, fruits, insects, lizards, roots, birds, and even small mammals.

HABITAT
Unlike other monkeys, baboons spend most of their lives on the ground in the forest and the bush. Animals that live in trees are usually safer, because they face fewer predators. This makes scientists wonder why baboons choose to live on the ground.

PREDATORS
Leopards, cheetahs, lions, and wild dogs are the baboon's main predators. When a predator approaches, baboons let out a high shriek to warn other baboons in their group. When the alarm is heard, the baboons head for the safety of trees.

SCIENCE EXTRA
The members of a baboon group, which is called a troop, eat together, sleep together, and help clean each other. You might see baboons grooming—picking insects off of each other and using their fingers to comb each other's hair. When they do this, they look very human!

WHITE RHINOS

WHITE RHINOS are not really white. In fact, they're the same dark gray color as black rhinos. They're called white rhinos because they have big, wide lips, and the Afrikaans word for lips is *weit*.

PHYSICAL CHARACTERISTICS
Rhinos are the second-largest land animal, bigger than all others except the elephant. Adult rhinos stand six to seven feet tall and weigh up to eight thousand pounds, which is heavier than the average car.

PREDATORS
White and black rhinos are hunted by humans for their horns, which are used to make potions in some countries. However, there is no scientific evidence that the horns help cure any disease or ailment. Rhinos are an endangered species.

FOOD
Although rhinos might appear to be threatening, they eat only grass and plants. They use their dangerous-looking horns to dig up the plants they eat.

FUN FACT
A black rhino will charge if it's threatened, but a white rhino will simply curl up its tail and walk away.

BARBARY SHEEP

BARBARY SHEEP are mountain sheep. These gentle animals live where mountains meet the open grassland, which is called the savanna. During the day, Barbary sheep stay in the relative safety of the mountains, where they're able to climb nimbly about on rocks. When the sun sets, they venture down into the savanna to graze.

PHYSICAL CHARACTERISTICS

Both male and female Barbary sheep have horns, but the male's are much larger. Barbary sheep are known for their long manes, which begin like a beard at the throat and run along the breast down to their front legs.

DEFENSES

Because they're light-colored, Barbary sheep blend in with their surroundings. When predators approach, the sheep remain perfectly still. This makes Barbary sheep hard to see.

FUN FACT

When male Barbary sheep fight by locking their triangular horns, they're not really trying to hurt each other. Each male is trying to wrestle the other to the ground, just to show who's boss.

Our Lives as Photographers and Writers

We love to travel, and we love to take pictures of wild animals, interesting places, and fascinating people. Our travel assignments are educational experiences. But they're also a challenge, because each assignment requires special talents and equipment.

Our most recent African safari presented several challenges. Flying to Kenya and then Tanzania from New York took three days, so we were very tired when we finally arrived. In Tanzania, where we joined the safari, the roads were bumpy. We were bounced around all day, and so were our cameras.

Our "home" for the trip was a two-person tent on the African plains. The scenery was spectacular, but listening to nearby lions roar all night was a little scary! Then there was the outdoor shower. When the overhead water bag was filled with fresh water, hundreds of honeybees buzzed over our heads, looking for a drink. Many of them got a shower, whether they needed one or not.

When we took the 3-D pictures in this book, we used special cameras that have not been made since the 1950s. To make sure we got the best shots with this antique equipment, we photographed every scene using two identical cameras, just in case one was not working properly.

We hope you have a chance to go on a safari of your own someday. It's a wonderful, once-in-a-lifetime adventure.